This book belongs to

_____

© 2006 Big Idea, Inc.

VEGGIETALES®, character names, likenesses, and other indicia
are trademarks of Big Idea, Inc. All rights reserved.

All scripture quotations, unless otherwise indicated, are taken from the
HOLY BIBLE, NEW INTERNATIONAL READER'S VERSION®.
Copyright © 1995, 1996, 1998 by International Bible Society.
All rights reserved.

Published by Scholastic Inc., 90 Old Sherman Turnpike, Danbury, Connecticut 06816.

No part of this work may be reproduced in whole or in part, or stored in a retrieval system,
or transmitted in any form or by any means, electronic, mechanical, photocopying, recording,
or otherwise, without written permission of the publisher.

SCHOLASTIC and associated logos are trademarks and/or
registered trademarks of Scholastic Inc.

This product is available for distribution only through the direct-to-home market.

ISBN: 0-7172-9963-5

Printed in the U.S.A.

First Scholastic printing, August 2006

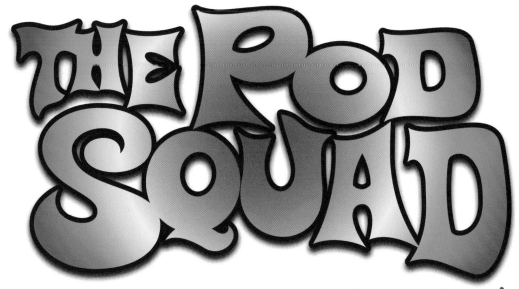

THE POD SQUAD

A Lesson in Using Nice Words

by Doug Peterson

Illustrated by Tod Carter and Joe Spadaford

SCHOLASTIC INC.

New York Toronto London Auckland Sydney
Mexico City New Delhi Hong Kong Buenos Aires

Ladies and gentlemen, the story you are about to read is silly. The names have been changed to protect the serious.

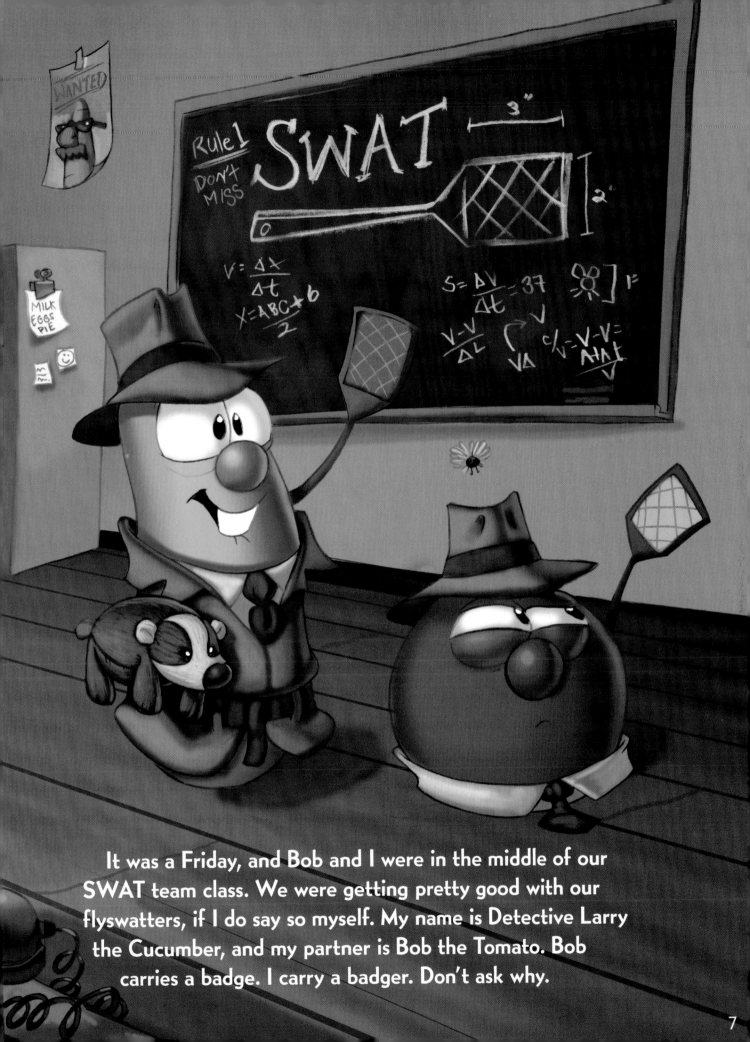

It was a Friday, and Bob and I were in the middle of our
SWAT team class. We were getting pretty good with our
flyswatters, if I do say so myself. My name is Detective Larry
the Cucumber, and my partner is Bob the Tomato. Bob
carries a badge. I carry a badger. Don't ask why.

Moments after I swatted a fly on Bob's head, the chief came in. He wanted us to teach three trainees how to be detectives. They were young, fresh, and straight out of Detective School. They were like peas in a pod. They called themselves The Pod Squad.

SWAT!

"They look more like the Odd Squad," I whispered to Bob.

"Hey, man, like what's happening?" said Jean-Claude.

"Peas, man," added Philippe.

"Right on," Gigi said.

Bob just rolled his eyes. He didn't feel like teaching new detectives. But orders were orders.

9

9:46 a.m. We got a call to go to Solomon Park, where a major mess had just happened.

"Let's get rolling!" I shouted.

"Man, like, let's take our car," suggested Gigi.

RING! RING!

The Pod Squad's plan sounded good to us—until we saw
their car. It was a big van covered with painted daisies and
wavy lines. But we didn't have time to change our minds.
So we piled into their van and took off.

9:52 a.m. The van broke down two blocks from headquarters.

Bob was furious and shouted, "This van is a piece of junk! Where did you get a clunker like this?"

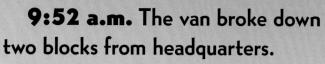

SPUTTER! POP!

"From the 1960s, man," said Philippe. Then he started singing, "How many miles can an old van go? The answer, my friend, is driving down the road. The answer is . . . "

Bob covered his ears. Don't know why, though, I thought the song had a good beat.

FIZZ!

13

10:10 a.m. We finally pushed the van to Solomon Park, where we found the mess.

"What happened here?" Bob asked Madame Blueberry, who ran a hot dog cart.

"Just the facts, ma'am."

"It was terrible!" said Madame Blueberry. "A crazy kid on a bicycle came tearing by. He knocked over my hot dog cart and just kept going!"

While Bob and I studied the mess, the three peas
stood around singing.

"Can you stop that singing for **one** second and
help out?" snapped Bob.

"Don't blow your cool, daddy-o," Gigi said.
"Like, what do you want us to do?"

DA, DA, DA

DEE, DEE, DEE!

I handed her a roll of yellow crime scene tape
and said, "Just do something with this."
The new recruits were **really** getting on our nerves.

10:24 a.m. We followed a trail of mustard for an entire block. It led to another huge mess.

WET CEMENT

"Oy! It was a crazy kid on a bike," grumbled Pa Grape. "He rode right through our wet concrete. I ask you—have you ever seen such a mess?"

Before we could answer, The Pod Squad came rushing up. Boy, they had done *something* with the crime scene tape all right. Jean-Claude had used the crime scene tape as a headband. Philippe used the tape as a strap for his guitar. And Gigi had completely wrapped herself up in the yellow stuff.

"That isn't what you're supposed to do with crime scene tape!" Bob shouted. "Can't you do *anything* right?"

They just looked at each other and started singing again— something about "Don't bring me down." I could tell Bob was losing it!

10:45 a.m. We followed a trail of concrete into Scooter's backyard. There, we found yet another mess. We also found the bicyclist, Li'l Pea, soaking wet. His bike was at the bottom of Scooter's pool.

"This kid came racing through my backyard," said Scooter. "He rode over my plants and right into my pool!"

"What do you have to say for yourself?" Bob asked Li'l Pea sternly.

"I'm s-s-s-s-sorry," said the freezing Li'l Pea. "I was just t-t-t-t-t-trying to learn how to ride a bike."

"It's all my fault, detectives," came a voice from behind. We spun around to see Laura Carrot. "I was supposed to be teaching Li'l Pea how to ride a bike," she said.

I made a note of that. "Go on," I said.

"Li'l Pea wasn't learning very fast, so I got angry and said some mean things to him," said Laura. "I was so frustrated that I gave Li'l Pea a super-big push. His bike went out of control and . . . well . . . you know the rest."

Bob sighed and said, "Laura, don't you realize how important it is to talk nicely when you're trying to help someone? That's called *encouragement*. Using mean words makes it hard to learn. It makes it . . . " Bob stopped in the middle of his sentence.

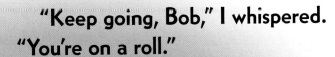

"Keep going, Bob," I whispered. "You're on a roll."

"But Larry, I just realized that *we* did the exact same thing as Laura!" said Bob. "We were supposed to teach The Pod Squad how to be detectives. But all we did was get angry and use mean words."

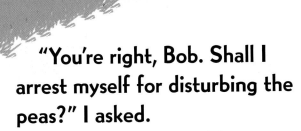

"You're right, Bob. Shall I arrest myself for disturbing the peas?" I asked.

"No, but God would want us to say we're sorry," Bob answered.

Suddenly Li'l Pea gave out a shout. "Hey! Look at me!" We all turned around and couldn't believe our eyes. Li'l Pea was riding the bike— with no hands!

While we had been talking with
Laura, The Pod Squad had pulled the
bike out of the pool. Then they had
taught Li'l Pea how to ride! But this
time, they had used *nice* words to do
it. They had *encouraged* Li'l Pea.

After sending Laura and Li'l Pea on their way, we spent the rest of the day showing Philippe, Jean-Claude, and Gigi how to be top-notch detectives. But this time, we used nice words. We built them up, instead of knocking them down. Then we all ended the day singing folk songs back at headquarters.

Over the next few days, The Pod Squad worked really hard.
When we actually gave them a chance, they learned quickly.
Within a week, they were full-time, first-rate detectives.
   Nice words made all of us better detectives. I guess all I am
saying is—give peas a chance.

. . . Pleasant words make people want to learn more.

Proverbs 16:21